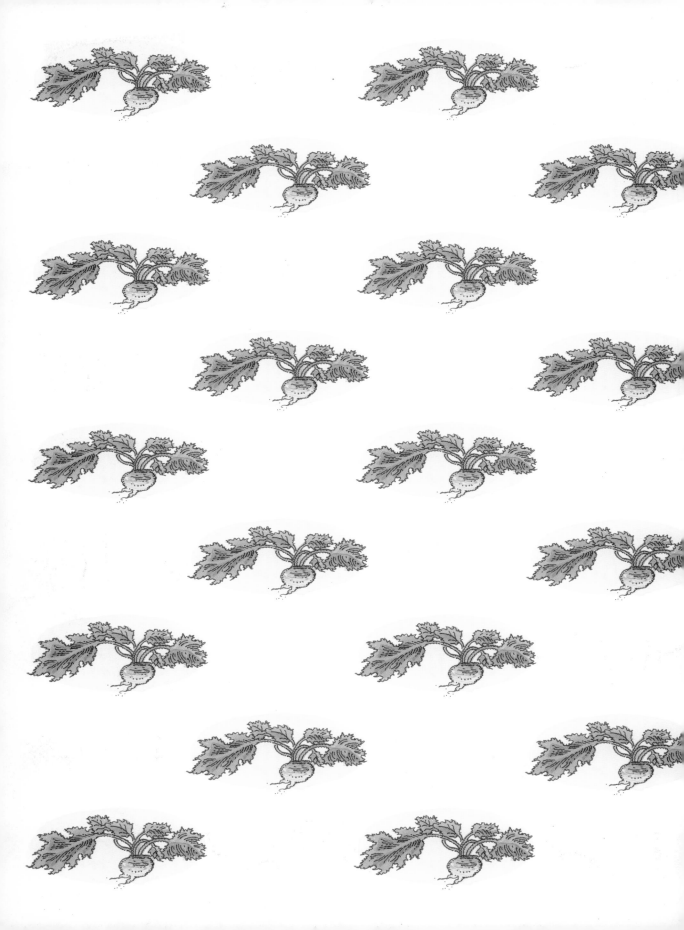

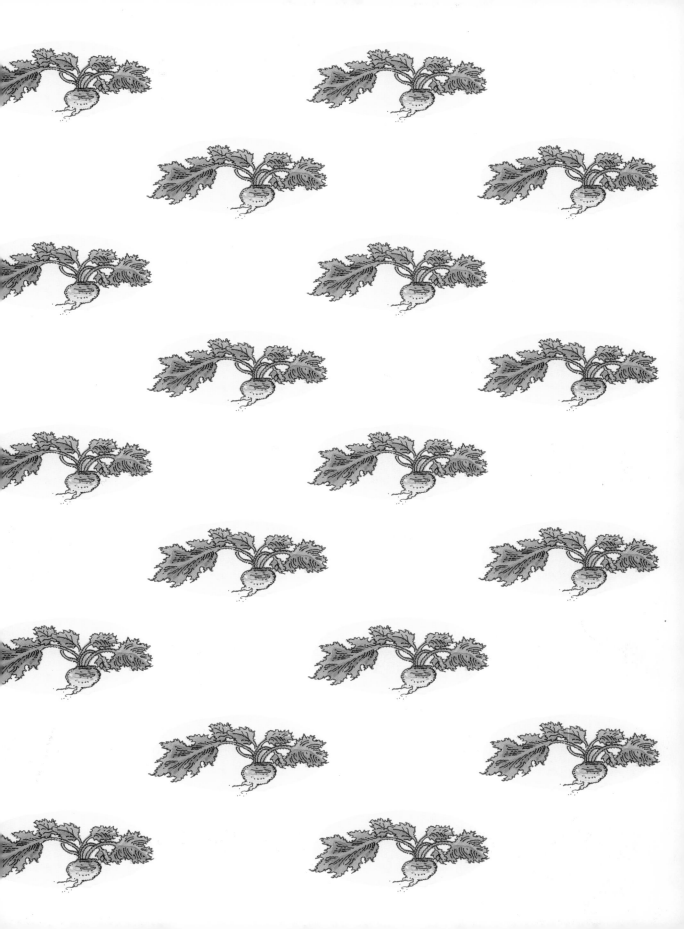

OXFORD
UNIVERSITY PRESS

Great Clarendon Street, Oxford OX2 6DP

Oxford University Press is a department of the University of Oxford.
It furthers the University's objective of excellence in research, scholarship,
and education by publishing worldwide in

Oxford New York

Auckland Bangkok Buenos Aires Cape Town Chennai
Dar es Salaam Delhi Hong Kong Istanbul Karachi Kolkata
Kuala Lumpur Madrid Melbourne Mexico City Mumbai Nairobi
São Paulo Shanghai Taipei Tokyo Toronto

Oxford is a registered trade mark of Oxford University Press
in the UK and in certain other countries

British Library Cataloguing in Publication Data available

ISBN 0 19 279149 4 Hardback
ISBN 0 19 279150 8 Paperback

1 3 5 7 9 10 8 6 4 2

Printed in China

The Enormous Turnip

Ian Beck

OXFORD
UNIVERSITY PRESS

Once upon a time, there was a little old man. He had a fine garden, where he grew all kinds of vegetables. He looked after his vegetables and treated them very kindly. He hoed the ground, and he kept the earth free from weeds and slugs. Everyone in the village said that his were the finest vegetables, best for colour and best for flavour.

Now, the little old man had a secret. When all his seeds were planted and the little seedlings were just popping their heads out of the ground, he would talk to them. And this is what he would say: 'Come on, you little seedlings, grow, grow!' He said it over and over, every evening before he went to bed.

Come on, you little seedlings, grow, grow!

His wife would shake her head and say that he was a fool – no good could come of talking to vegetables. She said that it was her careful watering that gave them such a fine crop.

One day the little old man planted out some turnips. His wife watered them well, and in time up popped the seedlings. 'Come on, you little seedlings, grow, grow!' said the old man, and grow they did.

One of them grew much bigger than the rest. It kept on growing, and growing, until it took up a whole corner of the garden.

Every morning the old man would come out and look at his turnip. He would give it a little pat, and talk kindly to it. The turnip kept on growing, until it took up half the garden.

One morning his wife said, 'It's time to pull up that great turnip – there's enough there to feed the whole village.'

So the old man went out and began to pull up the enormous turnip. He pulled and pulled, but it wouldn't move. The old man called out to his wife, and his wife came and she pulled at the old man, and the old man pulled at the turnip, but it wouldn't move.

So the wife fetched a boy who lived nearby, and the boy pulled at the wife, and the wife pulled at the old man, and the old man pulled at the turnip, but still it would not move.

So the boy went to fetch his little sister, and the little sister pulled at the boy, and the boy pulled at the wife, and the wife pulled at the old man, and the old man pulled at the turnip, but still it would not move.

So the little sister ran to fetch her dog, and the dog pulled at the little sister, and the little sister pulled at the boy, and the boy pulled at the wife, and the wife pulled

at the old man, and the old man pulled at
the turnip, but still it would not move.

So then the dog was sent to fetch his friend
the cat, and then the cat pulled at the dog,
and the dog pulled at the little sister, and
the little sister pulled at the boy, and the
boy pulled at the wife, and the wife pulled at
the old man, and the old man pulled at the
turnip, but still it would not move.

So then the cat was
sent to fetch her friend
the little mouse, and
then the mouse pulled
at the cat,

and the cat pulled
at the dog,

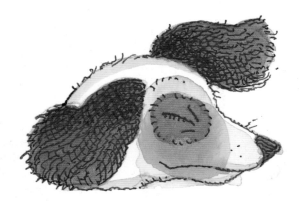

and the dog pulled
at the little sister,

and the little
sister pulled
at the boy,

and the boy
pulled at the wife,

and the wife pulled
at the old man,
and the old
man pulled
at the
turnip.

Whoosh! The turnip burst
out of the ground and the old
man fell on the wife, the wife fell

on the boy, the boy fell on the
little sister, the little sister fell
on the dog, the dog fell on the
cat, and the cat fell on the
little mouse, who said, 'Eeek!'

Eeek!

After they all brushed themselves down, they set to and made a great feast with the enormous turnip, and the whole village joined in and made a party of it.

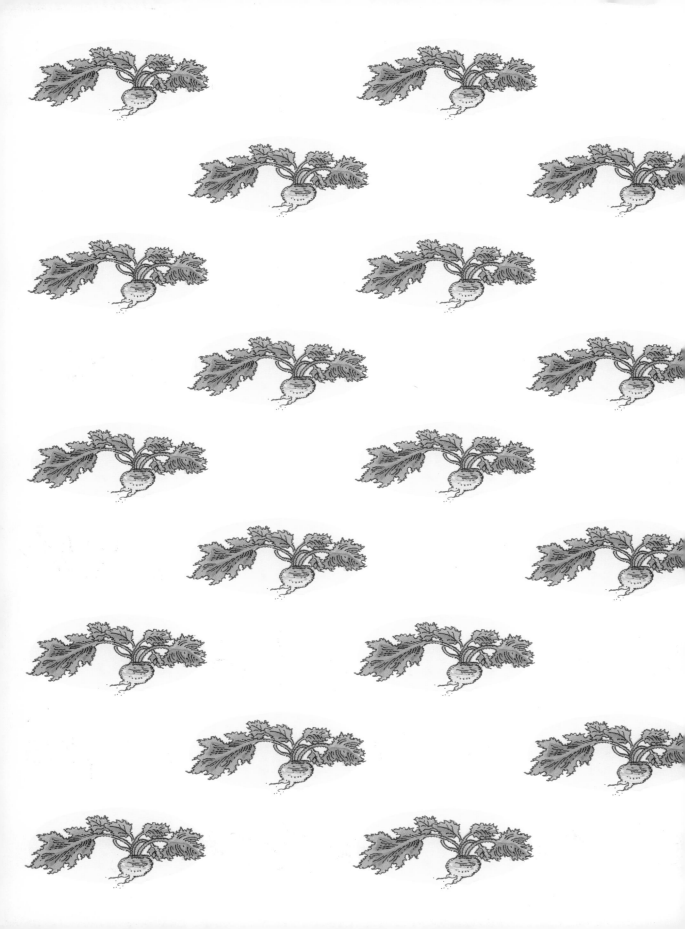

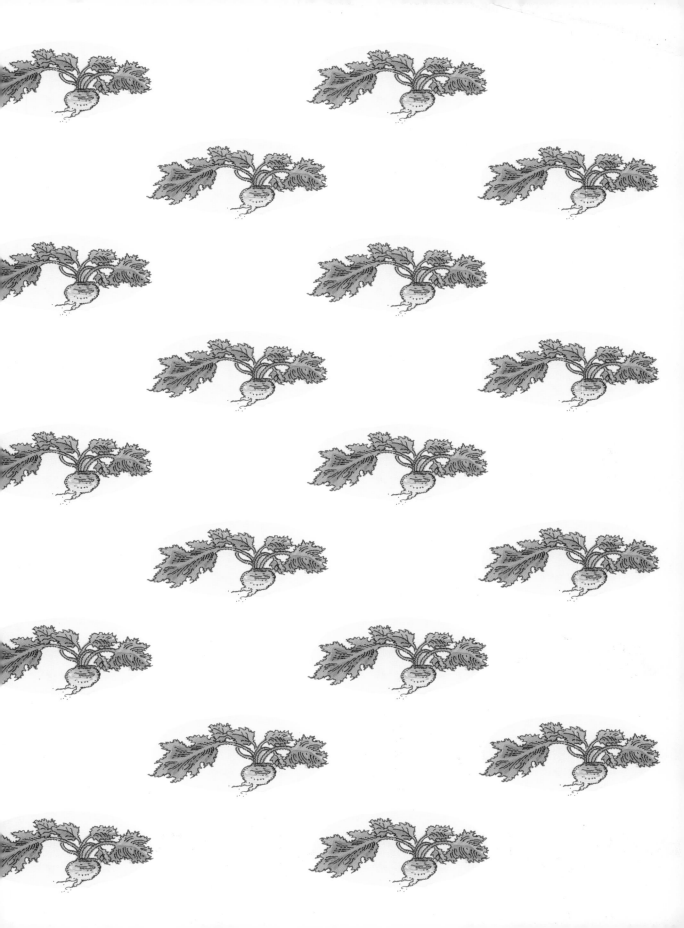